All Kids Should Play Team Sports

Annette Smith

Contents

Team Sports

I think all kids should play team sports.

My friend Jono and I
are in the same football team.
We play on a large sports field
not far from my home.

I didn't know Jono very well
before I joined the football team.
He lives on the other side of town.
Now, we are best friends.

3

Every Saturday, our parents take us to play a game against another team.

Before we start our game, we run up and down the field and practise our goal kicking.

Then, we line up in our teams and the **referee** tells us the rules so we remember them.

Everyone is excited.
We wish each other good luck.

Our parents watch us from the side lines.
They cheer for both teams.

Dance Groups

My cousin, Ellie, loves dancing.
She has been going to dance classes
for about three years.

Her teacher has started
a **hip-hop group**.
Ellie is always practising
the new dance moves.

Sometimes, the hip-hop group
dances at the shopping mall.
Everyone in the hip-hop group
tries their best.

Ellie knows that the dancing and music
will make people smile and feel happy.

Basketball Teams

William lives next door to my family.
He is in a basketball team.
The team practises on Tuesday
and Thursday evenings.

William always does his homework
before he goes to basketball training.

Lots of kids at William's school want to play in the basketball teams.

William works hard at shooting goals from all places on the court.

When William's team is in a match,
my parents take me to watch him play.
His mum and dad come with us
and we sit together in a group.

We all cheer when William
throws the ball into the hoop.
We always cheer when a player
in the other team gets a goal, too.

At the end of the game,
all of the players from both teams
shake hands.

Players in team games
know how to be fair when they play.

Relay Running

The teachers at our school say that we learn better if we are fit and healthy.

Our school has lots of team sports. In summer, we do **relay** running.

Many kids in our school like relay running.
We have six teams in my class.

Every week, our teacher mixes up the teams, so that we can run with fast runners and slower runners.

Team games help all of the kids to do well.

Team Sports Are Great

I think team sports are great
because they help kids to stay fit and healthy.

Team sports are the best way to meet kids
from other schools and to make new friends.

I am glad that I play a team sport
because I have fun
and learn many new things every day.

Glossary

hip-hop group (*noun*)
people who dance together to hip-hop music, which has strong beats

referee (*noun*) a person who makes sure that the rules are followed in a game

relay (*noun*) a race that is run by four or more people, who each take a turn